Christmas Mouseling

written by DORI CHACONAS

illustrated by SUSAN KATHLEEN HARTUNG

VIKING

On a cold December night when the north wind blew blustery and bold, a baby mouse was born. Mother Mouse held him close, and they snuggled deep into the nest.

"Please say 'Mama,'" she coaxed her new baby. But the winter mouseling only shivered and sneezed, *Ah-choo!*

"My poor, sweet mouseling!" Mother Mouse whispered. "It is so cold!"

Then, *whoosh!* the winter wind blew the tiny mouse nest apart.

Mother Mouse hugged her baby tighter and set out through the frosty night.

aa! Baa!" a sheep called from the shelter of a hillside.

"Oh, Sheep," Mother Mouse said. "I must find a warm place for my mouseling. He is newborn and cold, and he will not say 'Mama.'"

"A *baaad* time of year to be born!" said Sheep. "Use my grassy bed if you like. I'm on my way to see a king."

"A king?" Mother Mouse said. "What king?"

"*Baaah!*" said Sheep. "I don't know! I only follow the shepherd."

Sheep trotted off to join the flock.

Mother Mouse nestled her baby into the dried grass of Sheep's bed.

But . . .

The north wind blew. The snowflakes flew. And the mouseling sneezed, *Ah-choo! Ah-choo!*

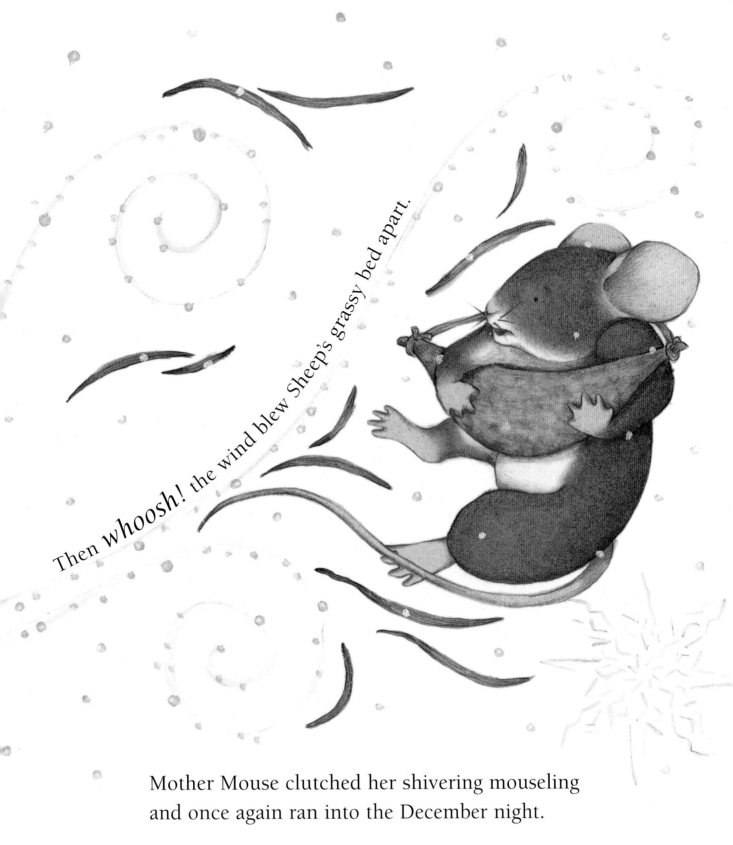

Then *whoosh!* the wind blew Sheep's grassy bed apart.

Mother Mouse clutched her shivering mouseling
and once again ran into the December night.

"*Cooo! Cooo!*" a dove called from a tree.

"Oh, Dove," Mother Mouse said. "I need a warm place for my baby. He is cold and sneezy, and he will not say 'Mama.'"

"Poor *coooey*," said Dove. "A blustery time of year to be born! You're welcome to use my nest. I'm on my way to see a king."

"You, too?" Mother Mouse asked. "How did you hear of a king?"

"Sheep told me," said Dove. And with that, Dove flew into the night.

Mother Mouse tucked her baby into Dove's feathery nest.

But . . .

The north wind blew. The snowflakes flew. And the mouseling sneezed, Ah-choo! Ah-choo!

Then *whoosh!* the wind blew Dove's feathery nest apart.

Mother Mouse once again carried
her baby into the night.

ooo! Mooo!" A cow lumbered out from behind a hedge.

"Oh, Cow," Mother Mouse said. "I need a warm place for my mouseling. He is tiny and shivery, and he will not say 'Mama.'"

"A chilly time of year to be born!" Cow said. "You can use my bed behind the hedge. I'm *moooving* off to see a king."

"Who is this king?" Mother Mouse asked.

"I do not know, but he must be very special," Cow answered. "Many are going to see him." Then she followed Sheep's footsteps across the hillside.

Mother Mouse bundled her baby into the deepest straw of Cow's bed.

But . . .

The north wind blew. The snowflakes flew. And the mouseling sneezed, Ah-choo! Ah-choo!

Then, whoosh! the winter wind blew Cow's straw bed apart.

Once more, Mother Mouse held her baby
tightly and went into the night.

The gusty wind whipped at her ears and
nipped at her tail.

The mouseling coughed . . .

and sniffled . . .

and sneezed . . .

Ah-choo!

Mother Mouse ran faster.

At last, from the top of a hill, Mother
Mouse looked down on a small wooden
shelter. It was surrounded by a halo of
light—a light so warm that she ran
down the hill to reach it.

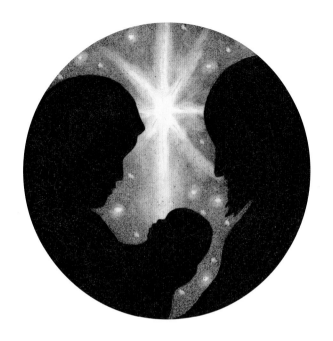

 o her surprise, Sheep was there. Dove was there. Cow was there. They all looked happy to be in this place.

"Maybe this night is too cold to look for a king," Mother Mouse said.

Others were there, too.

Donkey, Cat, Dog . . .

A man and a woman . . .

And a baby in a manger, covered with a soft, warm cloth.

"So warm!" Mother Mouse whispered.

ith her shivering baby in her arms, she crept into the end of the manger. Just then she noticed the woman watching her.

Mother Mouse grabbed up her mouseling, ready to run. But the woman's smile was gentle, and Mother Mouse knew she had no reason to be afraid.

"What a wonderful night to be born," the woman said.

Mother Mouse wrapped her baby in a corner of the soft, warm cloth.

The north wind blew. The snowflakes flew.

The mouseling did not sneeze, Ah-choo!

And the manger bed did not blow apart.

And so the mouseling snuggled more deeply into the manger.

Then the Christmas Mouseling opened his eyes and said, "Mama!"

For Stacy, my inspiration
—D. C.

For Ava
—S. K. H.

VIKING
Published by Penguin Group
Penguin Young Readers Group, 345 Hudson Street, New York, New York 10014, U.S.A.

Penguin Books Ltd, Registered Offices: 80 Strand, London WC2R 0RL, England

First published in 2005 by Viking, a division of Penguin Young Readers Group

1   3   5   7   9   10   8   6   4   2

Text copyright © Dori Chaconas, 2005
Illustrations copyright © Susan Kathleen Hartung, 2005
All rights reserved

LIBRARY OF CONGRESS CATALOGING-IN-PUBLICATION DATA
Chaconas, Dori, date-
Christmas mouseling / by Dori Chaconas ; illustrated by Susan Kathleen Hartung.
p.   cm.
Summary: When her shivering baby is born on a cold winter night, a mouse follows some animals
to a special manger where she receives help from another mother.
ISBN 0-670-05984-6 (hardcover)
1. Jesus Christ—Nativity—Juvenile fiction. [1. Jesus Christ—Nativity—Fiction.
2. Christmas—Fiction. 3. Mice—Fiction. 4. Mother and child—Fiction. 5. Animals—Fiction.]
I. Hartung, Susan Kathleen, ill. II. Title.
PZ7.C342Chr 2005
[E]—dc22
2005004458

Manufactured in China
Set in Berkeley
Designed by Kelley McIntyre